SDrury

22-82

THE PIRATES OF PUDDING BEACH

THE PIRATES OF PUDDING BEACH

Saviour Pirotta

Illustrated by Chris Riddell

MACMILLAN CHILDREN'S BOOKS

First published 1989 by
MACMILLAN CHILDREN'S BOOKS
A division of Macmillan Publishers Limited
London and Basingstoke
Associated companies throughout the world

ISBN 0–333–51085–2

A CIP catalogue record for this book is available from the
British Library

Typeset by Matrix, 21 Russell Street London WC2

Printed in Hong Kong

for Michael, my brother

Author's Note

This book is a work of fiction but is based on the real history of the pirates in the Mediterranean sea.

The pirate Captain Dragut really did exist. His exploits in many countries earned him the wrath of the Knights of Saint John. Although the trip to Ragusa only took place in the writer's imagination, the Knights did destroy Captain Dragut's fleet in 1565. The actual location of the battle, however, was Malta.

Toni Bayada too was a real person. He is still regarded as a hero by the Maltese.

Yusuf Sayid is a fictional character. The grave in the cave described in the early chapters of the book belongs to an unknown pirate.

S.P.

1. The Cave under the Cliffs

For weeks Salvu Sant had been waiting for a letter from his friends in England. He stood on the edge of the cliff and watched the postman chugging up the steep road on his ancient motorbike.

"Is there any *posta* for me?" he called.

The postman nodded and Salvu rushed down to meet him. "It's a letter from England," said the postman, stopping his bike in the shade of a fig tree.

"It *has* to be from Lottie and Mark," Salvu said breathlessly. "I've been waiting to hear from them for almost a month."

The postman rummaged around in his pouch and found a rather crumpled blue envelope. "Are they coming to see you again?" he asked.

Salvu nodded. "Dad invited them for three weeks starting August the twenty-fifth. I hope they can make it."

1

The postman handed him the letter and Salvu looked at the postmark. "It took five days to get here," he complained. "No wonder this country's going to the dogs."

The postman laughed. "Well, are you going to keep the contents of that letter a secret, or what?" he said.

Salvu opened the envelope carefully and skimmed through the letter. "They *are* coming," he cried. "They've booked their flights already."

"That's great," the postman said. "Maybe now you'll stop hassling me for a while."

Salvu grinned and tucked the letter in the back pocket of his denim shorts. "I'm sorry," he said.

"That's all right," the postman laughed as he kick-started his motorbike. "I was only joking."

Salvu nodded and started back home. It was almost ten now and the sun was getting hot.

At the top of the cliff, he stopped for a rest. In front of him the road crossed a large car park towards Maria's Guest House – the ancient, rambling villa where he and his father lived and worked. To his right, a low rubble wall marked the edge of a cliff that overlooked Gozo Harbour. To his left, the rocks dropped straight to Pudding Beach with only an old iron fence to keep cars and people from going over the edge.

Salvu turned and looked over the railings. Below him Pudding Beach was deserted. Above it, the high rocks were pockmarked with caves and DANGER: NO CLIMBING signs. Salvu smiled. The highest of those caves was the secret hideout he shared with Lottie and Mark. No one from the beach could reach it. And no one in the guest house knew there was a secret passage that stretched all the way from the cellar to the back entrance of the cave.

Salvu kicked a pebble lazily with his foot and watched it tumble down the cliffs. Then he wiped his face with a handkerchief and went home.

Guests nodded and smiled to him as he wandered through reception. Salvu returned their greetings and made for the kitchen.

His father was nowhere around. Salvu went to a noticeboard on the wall and found a note. "Salv," he read. "I've gone over to the greengrocers for some melons. I'll be back at eleven. Please chop lettuce and cucumber for salads. *Grazzi*. Dad."

Salvu pinned the note back on the board and grinned. He had nearly an hour to visit the hideout. Quickly, he closed the kitchen door and went down into the cellar.

It was quite dark among the old barrels, sacks of root vegetables and piles of rubbish. Salvu switched on a torch. Then he picked his way among the empty beer crates and came to an old, broken fridge by the far wall.

A couple of mice scuttled away frantically as

3

Salvu jiggled the old machine to test its wheels. He waited a moment. When the mice were gone, he pushed the fridge to one side and revealed a trapdoor set in the floor.

A large spider crawled out of the keyhole. Salvu brushed it aside with his foot and took a penknife from his pocket. Slowly, he forced the trapdoor open. Then he shone his torch into the hole.

The light fell on a flight of stairs. Salvu tested the first step with his foot. It was wet and slippery with moss. He opened the fridge and exchanged his new trainers for a pair of old climbing boots.

Carefully, he picked his way down the steps and felt around for a metal rail. When he found it, he pulled on a rope above his head and the trapdoor slammed shut.

The echo of the crash was deafening. Salvu waited until it died. Then he shone his torch down the tunnel. Bats and spiders glared back at him with large, angry eyes. Salvu ducked under the cobwebs and hurried along the passage until he passed under an ancient arch. In less than five minutes he found himself in the cave overlooking Pudding Beach.

"Helloo-wow." Salvu's call echoed around the walls and bounced off the rocks. The boy looked around him. From the roof of the cave, hundreds of glittering stalactites reached down almost to the sandy floor. At the far end, sunlight streamed through the mouth of the cave. Salvu walked over to the light and looked out.

Far below, a fisherman's boat was moving lazily across the water. Two dolphins poked their heads out of the sea and yakked. Salvu whistled and called. "Hiss, boo, what are you doing here?"

The dolphins wagged their heads, then disappeared. Salvu laughed. Suddenly the fisherman looked up. Salvu shrank back into the cave and set to work.

By the archway there was an old treasure chest. Salvu opened it and pulled out several pirate costumes. Ugghh – they were full of dust and spiders. Salvu went to an old barrel behind the stalactites and found a plastic basin and some washing powder. He filled the basin with water from an ancient hogskin, threw in a handful of soap and washed the costumes. Then he spread them out on the rocks to dry.

Going back to the treasure chest, he found three grimy swords.

"I can't expect Mark and Lottie to use rusted weapons," Salvu said to himself. "I'll have to smuggle them back home and give them a good polish."

He rummaged in the chest some more and found an old telescope with a broken lens. "This will have to be repaired too," Salvu thought. So he fetched a piece of twine from the barrel and tied the swords and the telescope together. Then he slung them on his back and started towards the tunnel.

As he reached the archway, Salvu heard the sound of a ferry boat approaching the harbour. "*Istra*", he said out loud to himself. "It's half past eleven already. I'd better get started on those salads."

Quickly, he made his way along the tunnel and hurried up the steps. The trapdoor did not creak again as he opened it.

"*Sawwa*," said Salvu to himself. "I won't need to oil it again."

He pushed the fridge back in place and put the boots, the swords and the telescope inside it. Then he looked around for a sack of cucumbers. As he found it, his father opened the cellar door.

"Salvu, have you started on those salads yet?" he asked.

"I'm just about to," replied the boy.

He put some cucumbers in a colander and took them out to the back yard to scrub under the pump. High above him an Air Malta plane thundered across the sky. Salvu looked up.

"Roll on fifteenth of August," he whispered to himself. I can't wait to go looking for buried treasure again."

YUSUF SAYID
A FIERCE PIRATE
MURDERED BY HIS OWN CAPTAIN
OLAF DRAGUT
ON THE 26th of AUGUST
1565
MAY GOD HAVE MERCY
ON HIS SOUL.

2. The Haunted Well

Salvu shielded his eyes with his right hand and looked out to sea. A large ferry boat with two funnels was approaching the harbour.

"Hiy-a there," Salvu called. "Can anyone see me?"

Some children on the boat pointed to him and waved. Salvu wondered if Lottie and Mark were amongst them.

All around him the quay was starting to fill up with people. Taxi drivers squabbled with policemen to get nearer to the waterfront. Children ran up and down the concrete, waving and shouting greetings.

The ferry boat entered the harbour and a surge of foam drifted towards the shore, making the moored fishing boats tremble. Salvu saw the people on board dash down to their cars on the lower deck. On the quay, two men in overalls came forward and signalled to the skipper with small, white flags.

The boat drew up to its moorings. Thick ropes were hurled from the decks and fastened to large bollards in the quay. Then the ramps were lowered and passengers started to spill down them.

Mr Sant's blue van was one of the first to come out. Salvu rushed forward to meet it.

"Hiya there, sailor," said a voice.

Salvu peered into the van and saw two white faces grinning happily from ear to ear.

"Hey, it's two dead fish," he teased.

One of the faces bent forward and opened the passenger door. "Climb aboard, pirate," said Lottie.

Salvu squeezed into the van and sat on top of the luggage. "Welcome to Gozo, corpses," he said. "Had a nice flight to Malta?"

"Yes, thank you," said Mark.

"The trip to Gozo was nicer though," Lottie added.

"I need to get some melons for lunch," Mr Sant said as he drove out of the harbour. "Do you mind if we go and fetch them now?"

" 'Course not," said Mark. "We'd love to see some countryside."

Mr Sant drove past the cliffs and took a wider road towards the open country. In no time at all they were bumping along a narrow dirt track towards a small farm.

"It isn't half hot," Lottie complained. "I feel like a fried chip already."

"It's going to get worse," warned Mr Sant. "You'd better invest in some sun tan oil, you two."

Mark held up a plastic bottle. "We got some already."

"I'd use it too if I were you," Salvu said. "Otherwise we'll have to rub your burnt skin with fresh tomatoes."

Lottie dug him painfully in the ribs. "We're not standing for any of your witch medicine this year, Dr Frankenstein."

"It's not witch medicine," Salvu insisted. "It's alternative therapy."

Mr Sant swung the car into a farmyard and parked under a vine.

"Here we are," he said. "I won't be a moment."

Mark watched him leave the car and disappear round the side of the old farm. Then he turned to Salvu.

"Is the cave ready?" he asked.

"All systems go." Salvu nodded proudly. "I've washed the costumes and polished the cutlasses. I found an old map, too. It might come in handy if we decide to do a spot of treasure hunting."

Somewhere behind the farm a dog started to bark ferociously. Lottie looked out of the window. "Hey, what's that little hideaway over there?" she asked.

10

Salvu gestured towards a small cave surrounded by prickly pears and figs. "That's the well of Yusuf Sayid," he said. "It's supposed to be haunted."

Mark giggled. "Who by?"

"Yusuf Sayid, stupid. He was a famous pirate. Come on, let's take a look."

They left the car and climbed over the farmyard wall towards the little cave. Behind the farm, the dog's ferocious barking stopped.

"Are we allowed to go in there?" Lottie said.

"It doesn't belong to anyone in particular," Salvu replied. "And we're not doing any harm, are we?"

11

Half expecting someone to come out at them, the three tiptoed into the cave. Somewhere behind the rocks, water was dripping into a hidden pool. Nettles nodded in the cool breeze.

"Look," said Lottie, pointing to a large pit marked out with white paint. "That must be the well."

"And that's the pirate's grave," said Salvu, nodding at a tombstone at the other end of the cave.

Mark walked over to the grave. "Where's this ghost, then?"

"It only comes out once a year," Salvu replied. "No one knows when."

Mark brushed weeds away from the crumbling stone. "Hey," he said. "There's something written on it."

Salvu bent down for a closer look. The inscription was full of moss and dust but the children could still read the message clearly:

YUSUF SAYID
A FIERCE PIRATE
MURDERED BY HIS OWN CAPTAIN
OLAF DRAGUT
ON THE 26TH OF AUGUST 1565
MAY GOD HAVE MERCY ON HIS SOUL

"That's creepy," said Lottie. "Who'd erect a tombstone for a pirate?"

"Legend has it that some children did," Salvu replied. "No one knows exactly who they were."

"I must take a picture of this," Mark said. "Where's the Polaroid?"

Lottie dug in her bag and found a camera. Salvu stood up and brushed the moss from his knees.

"Stand back, everyone," Mark said. He pointed the camera at the grave and pressed a button.

"You haven't got it right," Lottie said. "The weeds are blocking out some of the words."

"I'll take another, then." Mark slung the camera over his shoulder and started pulling up the weeds.

Just then Mr Sant called them.

"We're coming," Salvu called back.

Quickly, Mark fiddled with the knobs on his camera and pressed the button again. "Got it."

"Right, then, let's go."

They left the cave and crossed the field towards the blue van. Soon they were speeding along the road towards home.

"Hooray," shouted Lottie, as the van started the painful climb up the cliff. "We're here."

3. A Rusted Lamp

"Can we go to our cave now?" Lottie asked.

Salvu shook his head. "I'm afraid Dad's expecting a delivery of onions this afternoon. He'll be in and out of the cellar all the time."

The three friends were sitting on the verandah of the guest house. After unpacking and a quick shower, Mr Sant had served them a special meal of pumpkin stew and melon ice-cream. Now they were alone, free to do as they pleased until dinnertime.

"Let's go for a swim, then," Mark said.

They fetched their bathing costumes and started down the cliff. The ground was burning hot under their feet and the tarmac smelt faintly of burning rubber.

"Look at those cool waves," Lottie said longingly. "It makes you want to dive into the water from here, doesn't it?"

14

"It sure does," Salvu said. "Come on, I'll race you both to the beach."

He took off his flipflops and raced down the cliff path towards the cool, blue sea. Mark and Lottie followed.

"Last one to hit the water is a funny dolphin," Mark called. Salvu threw his flipflops on to the rocks and made for the water.

"Don't forget to take off your watches, boys," Lottie warned.

Mark stopped to check his watch and Lottie – who had cunningly left her watch at the guest house – gave a flying leap into the sea.

"I win," she shouted triumphantly through mouthfuls of salty water.

"That's cheating," Mark complained, following her and Salvu. Lottie giggled and snorted bubbles through her nose.

"Isn't this wonderful?" she sighed. "I can see the starfish at the bottom of the sea."

"I'm going to sunbathe," Mark said. "You coming, Salv?"

Salvu squeezed water out of his eyes and licked his lips. "Nah, the beach looks too hot for me," he said. "I think I'll go snorkelling instead."

Mark and Lottie clambered on to a hot dry rock and found a nice, smooth patch they could lie on. Lottie fetched the bottle of sun tan lotion from her bag.

"I'd use it generously, if I were you," Salvu

said, climbing expertly on to the rocks without looking for footholds. "You two look like a pair of boiled lobsters already."

He pulled his snorkel out of his bag and rinsed it in the sea. Then he put on his flippers.

"Beware of sea monsters, sailor," Mark laughed.

Salvu grinned and adjusted the snorkel on his face. "See you in Atlantis," he joked.

Mark and Lottie groaned. Salvu waded into the shallows, then struck out towards the open sea with his face under water.

All around him, the rays of the afternoon sun shimmered like pure gold. Giant crabs moved lazily across the rocks. Tiny seahorses stared with huge, bulging eyes.

Salvu stopped to examine the coral. Below him, a large octopus waved its tentacles. A shoal of black fish came swimming by. Salvu waited for them to pass. Then he took a deep breath and dived towards the seabed.

Suddenly a moray eel flashed out of a hole. Knowing its fins were deadly, Salvu made no attempt to touch it. The eel snapped at a squid and disappeared among the seaweed, its flat tail quivering.

Salvu surfaced for air. On the beach, Lottie and Mark seemed to be dozing. He adjusted his snorkel and dived again.

This time he saw no fish. A couple of shells closed up as he passed by, and a starfish waved

16

its five legs. But there were no mullets or crabs. Salvu was rather alarmed. What could the reason be?

Suddenly he remembered. Of course, small fish always disappeared when big predators were around. Salvu wondered what big fish could be lurking around Pudding Beach? Could it be a tuna? Or, worse, a shark? Wishing he'd listened to the radio warnings before coming to swim, he started paddling furiously towards the shore. Once or twice he stopped to look around him. There was no sign of the big fish anywhere, but the smaller creatures of the sea were still absent.

In less than five minutes, Salvu felt seaweed brush his chest. Good, that meant he was in very shallow water. Big fish could not follow him here. He breathed a sigh of relief and clambered on to the rocks.

A moment later, he heard a sound at his feet. He looked down. A dolphin was churning the water with its fin.

"Hiss," he gasped. "What are you doing here?"

The dolphin half rose out of the water. "Yak, Yak, Yak," it said.

Salvu laughed. "Are you telling me the big fish is gone?"

The dolphin wagged her head.

"Clever girl," Salvu said.

The dolphin fell back into the water with a splash. Salvu left his snorkel on the rocks and jumped in after her. "Come on, you big monster," he laughed. "Take me for a ride. Let's see how fast you can go."

The dolphin let him catch hold of her fin, then arched her back and headed towards the harbour. A mischievous gleam came to her eyes. "Hold on," Salvu shouted, his mouth filling with water. "I'm not wearing my snorkel."

The dolphin ignored his plea and dived under the surface. Salvu's eyes and mouth clamped shut instinctively. He felt cold water rushing up his nose and pressing painfully on his ear drums.

The dolphin straightened her tail and dived deeper. Salvu grimaced and counted to five. Then he forced himself to relax. The water up his nose stopped tickling as if by magic. The painful drumming on his ears eased.

Hiss stayed underwater for what seemed like an eternity. She carried Salvu through a patch of tall, sticky seaweed and then cut through a cold current. Salvu shivered. Suddenly the dolphin arched her tail and surfaced again.

"Thanks, Hiss," Salvu spluttered, gasping for air and squeezing salt water out of his nose. "That was some ride."

The dolphin wagged her fin and disappeared under water. Salvu looked around him. He was floating in a huge dome-like cave behind the cliffs. High above him, the roof was packed with colourful stalactites. Salvu heard water dripping into the sea and wondered if it was fresh.

"Hiss," he said. "I never knew this cave existed. How did you bring me in here?"

The dolphin surfaced and splashed water in his face. Salvu laughed. Then he saw a large shadow looming at the back of the cave.

"Hiss," he called. "It's a wreck."

The dolphin nudged him with her lips and swam playfully towards the old schooner. Salvu followed her.

The wrecked ship was tilting at a crazy angle. One side was completely immersed in the sea while the other side was staring up at the roof of the cave. The prow and most of the deck rail were gone, but the three masts reached out among the stalactites like the stiff fingers of an old skeleton.

Salvu rapped on the wood with his knuckles. Most of the boards seemed to be solid. Salvu found a rusted chain hanging from the deck and pulled on it. It held.

Carefully, he hoisted himself up on to the deck. The slanting boards were slippery and covered in green slime. Salvu sat on a patch of moss and let gravity pull him to the centre mast.

In the water, the dolphin started to call.

"Coming," Salvu shouted back. Carefully, on his hands and knees, he made his way along the ship to the first cabin. There was nothing inside it. Salvu held on to the door frame, stood up and passed by the foremast towards the prow. Then he saw a large, gaping hole in the deck and looked down into it.

The water was too murky to see properly. Salvu could make out what looked like pieces of rotten furniture. Beside them were two rusted metal things like a church bell and a cannonball. Salvu found a piece of wood and threw it at them. The rotten furniture moved, and a slimy grey octopus peeped out from behind it.

"Ugh." Salvu backed away from the hole and

worked his way up to the edge of the deck again.

"Yak, yak, yak." Hiss was getting impatient now and was on the verge of leaving him behind.

"Hold your sea-horses," Salvu laughed, diving into the water and swimming around to the front of the ship. "Hiss," he joked. "Can you read the ship's name?" The dolphin wagged her head as if to say yes. Salvu studied the prow carefully. "T-H-E G-R-O-W . . . " Suddenly he stiffened. "Hiss," he called. "We've found the *Growling Dragon* – Captain Dragut's famous ship!"

The dolphin swooped past him, and Salvu caught hold of her fin.

"Don't you ever take anything seriously?" he said. "Come on, let's go and tell the others what we've found."

The dolphin wagged her tail but didn't move.

"Come on, Hiss," Salvu begged. "I want to get out."

The dolphin yakked, then dived towards the seabed. Salvu let go of her fin and followed. There was a rusted object lying in the seaweed.

Salvu scooped it up in his hands and brought it to the surface. "Look, Hiss," he said. "You found us an old pirate lamp."

4. *The Dragon Growls*

"So whose lamp was it?" Mark asked.

The three were sitting in their cave at last, eating ship's biscuits by moonlight and taking turns at cleaning Salvu's latest discovery.

"It must have belonged to Captain Dragut," Salvu said. "I found it near his wreck."

Mark scratched remnants of seaweed from the lamp and frowned. "How could that be?" he asked. "I read in the book you sent me for Christmas that Captain Dragut's ship was blown up in Sicily by the Knights of Saint John."

"Perhaps Captain Dragut had two *Growling Dragons*," Salvu suggested.

Lottie poured some oil on her cleaning rag. "It doesn't really look like a pirate's lamp, does it?" she said. "I think it would be more at home in Aladdin's cave."

22

"Aladdin's lamp was brass," Salvu said. "This is pottery. Very old, I should think."

"Wasn't Captain Dragut the guy who did Yusuf Sayid in?" asked Mark, looking up from his polishing.

Lottie put down the oil can and sighed impatiently, eager to get her hands on the lamp. "He must have been. We saw his name on the gravestone, didn't we?"

Salvu took the lamp from Mark and started rubbing it vigorously. The oil was seeping into the clay now, rubbing away the grime that had collected through the years.

"Captain Dragut was quite a bloodhound, I'm afraid," Salvu said. "In fact, I don't think there's an island in the Mediterranean that wasn't attacked by him. He ransacked Maria's Guest House once, too."

"You're kidding!" Mark gasped.

"I'm not." Salvu grinned proudly at his friends. "It wasn't a guest house then, of course. It was just a villa, one of the richest on the island. My ancestors were very wealthy, you know, until Captain Dragut stole their treasure and left them penniless. That's when they turned the villa into a guest house."

"The beast," said Lottie, not quite sure if Salvu were pulling their leg or not. "What did he do with the treasure?"

"I suppose he buried it somewhere." Salvu

shrugged thoughtfully and started to fill the lamp with oil. "He didn't get much time to enjoy his loot though. The *Growling Dragon* was blown up soon afterwards."

"Fancy living in a home that was attacked by pirates," Lottie said. "Just wait until I tell my friends back home."

"What I can't understand," wondered Mark, "is how the *Growling Dragon* was hauled intact into the cave?"

"There must have been an earthquake or a powerful storm." Salvu said. "We should inspect the wreck together tomorrow. Maybe we can find some clues."

"We should." Lottie stood up and went to the barrel for some more biscuits. Salvu put the lamp on top of the chest.

"Let's see if it works," Mark said. "Can you bring some matches, please, Lot?"

Lottie came back with a box and sat between the two boys. Mark gave the lamp one last flick with the cleaning rag. "You do the honours, Salv," he said. "You're the one that found the thing, after all."

Carefully, Salvu lit a match and held it to the wick. At first nothing happened. The match burnt down to his finger and died out. He lit another one and held it closer. This time a tiny yellow flame spluttered into life.

"It works," Lottie whispered triumphantly.

24

The flame turned green, shuddered and threw black shadows on the children's faces.

Lottie passed her finger through it and tapped the lamp lightly with her nails.

"I've never seen a lamp with a green light before," she said to Salvu. "Is there something in the oil?"

Salvu shook his head. "I don't think so."

Suddenly Mark jumped up. "Did you feel that?" he said.

The others looked puzzled. "Feel what?"

"The cave is swaying. Stand up and you'll feel it too."

Salvu and Lottie scrambled to their feet and stood as still as statues. Mark was right. They too could feel a faint, rocking movement under them.

"It's an earthquake," Lottie gasped.

"It can't be," Salvu said. "An earthquake causes a quick, short tremor, not a gentle sway. This feels as if we're on a boat."

"Look," shouted Mark who was peering around him in alarm. "The stalactites have disappeared."

Salvu looked up. Mark was right again. They could see no stalactites or glinting drops of water any more.

"Maybe the moon's gone in," Lottie said. "Or there's an eclipse or something."

Mark shook his head. "It's still shining through the mouth of the cave. Look."

Lottie turned to the light. "Hey," she said. "The entrance has changed too."

The boys looked at one another, unsure of what to do next. "It's a porthole," Lottie gasped in a mousy voice stifled by fear. "We seem to be on a ship. What do we do now?"

Before either of the boys could say anything, they heard voices. Instinctively, the three of them crouched behind the pirate chest and held their breath. The voices outside paused for a moment. Then someone threw open a door and stepped into the cave. Mark turned to Salvu.

"There is no door in the archway, is there?" he said in a whisper that sounded more like a shout in the silence. Salvu glared at him and held a finger to his lips. Mark bowed his head.

The man by the door started to speak again. The children couldn't understand what he was saying, but Salvu guessed he was speaking in Arabic. Another voice outside barked an order. The man closed the door, and the children heard two sets of footsteps fading away.

"I can't understand what's going on," said Salvu, coming out from behind the chest. "But I think Lottie's right. We're on a ship."

"What kind of ship?" Mark was not sure if it was fear or excitement that was making his skin feel hot and itchy.

"I have no idea," Salvu replied. "But it explains

26

the porthole, the door and the swaying, doesn't it?"

"The lamp must have done this," Lottie said. "Look, the flame has changed colour."

Salvu turned to the lamp and stared. The flame was an ordinary orange now, quivering in the breeze like any other light.

"Could it possibly be?" Mark wondered.

"There's an old temple not far from our house," Salvu said. "It used to be the Seat of Astarte, the goddess of life. People believed the priests of Astarte could make lamps whose light transported the faithful backwards and forwards through time."

"You mean like time machines?" Mark giggled despite his fear. "That's impossible."

"We're on a ship, aren't we?" Lottie said. "So there must be something in it. I say we explore a bit, to find out where we are."

The grin left Mark's face in an instant. "We can't," he gasped.

"Why not?" Lottie sounded scornful.

"Because we're on a pirate ship, dummy, that's why," Mark said. He pointed to a length of rope that lay in a heap on the floor. Beyond the rope was a half-open chest. It contained curiously curved swords and a large dagger.

"Scimitars," Salvu muttered. "We must be on an Arab schooner."

"I say we ought to go back." They could

hear the fear in Mark's voice now. Mark had never been one for doing dangerous things.

"You are a pair of softies," Lottie said scornfully. "Come on, we might never get the chance to explore a real pirate ship again."

"She's right," Salvu said. "But we must be careful. If we get caught we could be taken as slaves."

Mark said nothing but Lottie hurried to the door, opened it cautiously and peeped out. Outside was a long deck, with rigging on one side and barrels on the other.

The girl signalled the boys to follow her and made straight for a dark space behind the barrels.

"I think everyone except the night watch must be asleep," Mark whispered in the safety of their new hiding place.

"They must have someone on lookout, though," Lottie warned. "And a ship's cook often stays up late to bake bread for the morning."

Salvu stuck his head above the barrels and listened out for any sounds. There were none. "I think the coast is clear," he whispered at last. "Shall we explore some more?" The others signalled yes and Salvu led them along the deck. They kept to the shadows of the barrels, creeping forward on their hands and knees. Across the water the lights of the harbour shone in the darkness, and a merchant ship bobbed on the waves.

28

The children crept on. A few minutes later
they came to the open window of a cabin.
Carefully, Salvu raised his head and looked in.
The cabin was occupied. A well-built man was
sitting at a desk with his back to him. A small
monkey with a golden collar lay stretched out on
a sofa, seemingly asleep. The man was scribbling
in a large book. There was an inkwell at his elbow,
and a large map trailing from the desk to the
floor.

Salvu tried to see which countries were drawn
on it. Just then the breeze rustled the quills on
the desk. The man swore softly to himself and

turned to close the window. Salvu ducked, his heart beating like a drum.

When the window was closed, Salvu motioned the others to follow him and they worked their way towards the stern. Soon they came to a railing that marked the end of the deck. Salvu heard voices below them and guessed that the night watchmen were talking to the lookout. With his right hand, he signalled the others to stop. Then he crept forwards and looked down into the stern.

Two of the men below him carried long scimitars and wore the colourful tunics of Arab traders. Only the moon diamonds pinned to their turbans gave them away as pirates. Salvu realised the schooner was disguised as a North African merchant ship awaiting cargo. The lookout sported a variety of rich but tattered clothes, which meant he was a mercenary who hired himself out to different ships. All three men were deep in conversation.

"I've had enough of this," the lookout was saying. "Three days we've been anchored here, looking for that wretched lamp that went down with the first ship in the storm. Anyone would think the divers Dragut hired were blind."

"Captain Dragut wants that lamp at all costs," one of the guards replied. "I guess we'll stay here until we find it."

"Not me," the lookout said. "My brother has

offered me a job with a band of mercenaries from Sardinia. He tells me they're planning something big, something that will have, how shall I say it . . . ? An 'explosive effect on the whole world'."

"I'm sure Captain Dragut will miss you," remarked one of the guards sarcastically.

"Captain Dragut has gone soft in the head," the lookout replied, stung. "Fancy paying a treasure like the Sant family's heirlooms for a lamp. People say there was enough gold and diamonds in that villa on the cliffs to fill the coffers of a king."

The guards chuckled knowingly and threw amused glances at each other.

"What's the joke?" the lookout said, catching their look. "Are you suggesting Dragut did not exchange the treasure for the lamp as everyone says."

"Captain Dragut never parts with any of his booty," one of the guards assured him. "Those wretched monks who sold him the lamp never got anything more expensive than a sword through the guts."

The lookout's eyes grew wide with awe and his voice sounded incredulous. "You mean the Sant's treasure could still be hidden on this ship?"

The guards shrugged teasingly. "You'll have to ask Yusuf Sayid that," one of them said. "He's the only one Captain Dragut entrusts with his secrets . . ."

Suddenly a roar cut through the pirates' conversation. The lookout stopped talking and the guards stiffened. A door beyond the foremast crashed open and bright light fell across the deck.

Lottie, Mark and Salvu dived behind a pile of sacks. Moments later, someone in big, heavy boots marched past them and descended the stairs. The children heard an angry voice bark out an order. The guards mumbled a reply. Then the owner of the boots came back and went to his cabin.

"We'd better go back now," Salvu whispered. "I think we've seen enough for one night."

Mark raised his head above the sacks and peered out. The deck seemed deserted again. Quickly, the children wormed their way behind the barrels and slipped into the cabin where the lamp was.

"Look," said Lottie to Salvu. "Our old chest has changed to match the rest of the cabin. There's something written on it."

Salvu picked up the lamp and held it close to the writing. *"Growling Dragon II"*, Lottie read. "That proves there *are* two *Growling Dragons*, doesn't it?"

Salvu nodded.

"The first one must have sunk here during the storm the lookout mentioned," Mark said. "And the other was blown up in Sicily. Since we've found the lamp Dragut is searching for, we must be on the one that was blown up."

Just then Salvu heard the watchmen returning. Quickly he brought the lamp to his face and blew the light out. The guards' footsteps stopped.

In the same instant, the floorboards under the children's feet turned to sand.

"We've made it," cried Mark happily. "We're back in our cave."

5. A Few Things Explained

"I still don't understand," Mark said, passing his hand through the sand on the cave floor. "How could we have gone back in time and come back at the very same moment we left?"

"It does make sense if you think about it carefully," Salvu explained patiently. "I read a book about time once. It said that everything in the universe is given its own time on a planet or in space. You and Lottie and I were scheduled to live on Earth in the twentieth century. We have so many years to live, so many things to do and places to visit. Then, at a specific time arranged beforehand, we die."

"You mean everything is planned for us?" Lottie gasped.

Salvu nodded. "It's called destiny," he said. "Now I think this lamp was scheduled to be on Earth in the sixteenth century. It was meant to stay alight until the *Growling Dragon* perished under water. Then it was supposed to go out."

"And it did." Mark was beginning to see the logic behind it all now. "Except we tampered with its destiny by lighting it. So its own time started ticking away again and we were drawn into it."

"That's incredible," Lottie gasped. "You mean that if I lay my hands on something from the stone age and start using it, I'll find myself in the time of the mammoths?"

"Of course not," Salvu laughed. "The lamp has special powers. It came from the temple of Astarte, remember? Astarte was the goddess of life itself. She had power over life and death. People believed Astarte could make animals and crops die in an instant. Or she could make a person come alive again. Her priests knew a lot about destiny which we don't know today."

Mark's love of history shone in his eyes. "Where did all their knowledge go?"

"Their sacred writings were destroyed by Christians in the first century A.D," Salvu quoted from one of his history lessons. "The worship of Astarte was an underground cult, you see. It was seen by many as a weird religion for a crazy few. The temple survived, of course, and so did a few of Astarte's worshippers. Images of her were still being made and sold during the time of Captain Dragut."

"Will we go back to the *Growling Dragon* if we light the lamp again?" Lottie wondered.

"I think so," Salvu said.

Lottie jumped up excitedly. "Then why don't we? We could hunt around the ship for Salvu's family treasure. We always wanted to look for a real treasure, didn't we?"

Mark shot a worried glance at Salvu. "We shouldn't," he said weakly. "After all, we don't know if the treasure is really on board or not."

"Oh, come on, you guys," Lottie insisted. "We wouldn't be in any danger or anything. All we'd have to do is leave one of us to guard the lamp while the other two went exploring. Then, if we didn't come back within half an hour, the guard could blow out the lamp and we'd find ourselves back in the cave."

"Sounds risky," Mark said. "We don't know enough about the lamp yet."

"And we'll never know unless we light it up again," Lottie cut in. "What do you think, Salv?"

"I think we should go," Salvu said. "But we'd have to be really careful. I wouldn't like to cross swords with Dragut."

Lottie grabbed the matches.

"Mark can guard the lamp this time," she said. "Salvu and I will look for the treasure."

6. *Back on the* Growling Dragon

The cabin on the *Growling Dragon II* was not quite the same as the children had left it. Even in the dark, they could see that the pirates had moved things around, piled coils of ropes under the porthole and filled the barrel with dried figs.

"Where do we start looking?" Lottie asked.

"I think we should try Captain Dragut's cabin first," Salvu replied. "Perhaps there is a map or a clue or something. As Mark said, we have no idea where the treasure is. It could be locked up in a vault right under our noses. Or it could be buried somewhere on Gozo. We'll just have to make up our minds as we go."

"I'll find a safe place to hide," Mark said.

He carried the lamp to the back of the cabin and squeezed himself between the wall and a barrel. Lottie and Salvu opened the door.

Outside, a sharp wind was pulling the rigging taut and making it hum like a banshee.

"We'll never hear anyone coming in this racket," Lottie whispered.

She and Salvu made straight for the passage behind the barrels they'd used earlier. Progress was easy. No one passed by. High above the masts seagulls screeched and an owl hooted. A church clock on the island struck one.

Lottie reached the cabin and motioned Salvu to stop. Slowly, she stood up. Captain Dragut's window was open. Lottie peeped in and saw him sitting at his table, a candle by his elbow. The monkey on the sofa opened one eye and grunted. Lottie ducked behind the barrels.

Salvu made some space for her to sit and the two of them waited in silence. Ten minutes passed. The wind dropped and the rigging hung still. A flock of seagulls settled on the ship's masts and tucked their heads under their wings. The owl hooted again.

Somewhere near the prow of the ship a door crashed open. Someone marched along the deck in bare feet. Lottie put her eye to a gap between two barrels and saw a young lad carrying a tray of food. A delicious smell of mulled wine and spices filled the air.

The lad knocked politely on the cabin door. "Your wine, *Sidi* Dragut," he called. Dragut opened the door and Lottie smelt a faint odour of stale rum and gunpowder mixed with the aroma of the wine.

"I'll take it with the men," the Captain barked.

The lad nodded and retreated with the tray towards the prow. Lottie saw Captain Dragut slam his door shut, the monkey on his shoulder. A key turned noisily in the lock. Then the pirate followed the lad and silence settled over the deck once more.

"Now's our chance," Salvu whispered.

Lottie stood up cautiously and looked around her. The deck was clear, save for the gulls on the railings. Salvu stood up too. Silently, the two of them approached the open window and climbed into the cabin.

"I've never seen anything so posh in all my life," gasped Lottie as her feet sank into pure tiger skin carpet. "Just look at those pictures."

Salvu looked around him. Captain Dragut's cabin was a rich place indeed. The walls were covered in beautiful paintings, probably stolen from a hundred different palaces around the world. The furniture was made of polished oak and oiled mahogany. Golden swords and guns hung on the walls and a velvet tablecloth with golden tassels covered Dragut's desk.

Lottie tiptoed to a cabinet and opened its drawers. "There's all kinds of stuff in here," she whispered. "Charts and things, see."

Salvu came over and started to look through

the papers. "They're only letters," he said. "Here's one from the Pope. It was probably stolen from a Spanish galleon."

"Aren't there any maps?" asked Lottie.

"Not here," Salvu said. "Let's try the desk."

Lottie hurried to the writing table and started rifling through the papers. "Nope," she said. "Just pictures of the sky at night."

"Maybe there is no map," Salvu wondered. "Let's look for a clue."

"Like what?" Lottie said.

"Like a hidden key to the treasure room or a note. Anything." He turned to a cupboard by the door and opened it. There was nothing inside except a few bottles of rum and a pistol.

"What about the pictures?" Lottie said. "Pirates were always pasting things behind pictures, weren't they?"

Salvu looked at the frames helplessly. "There's too many of them!" he cried. "We can't possibly look in each one."

"We can if we hurry," Lottie said adamantly. "You keep a lookout, I'll go through them one by one."

Salvu stationed himself by the window and Lottie started examining the frames, feeling the space between the canvas and the backing paper with her fingers.

"Someone's coming," Salvu said suddenly.

Lottie stepped away from the pictures and

looked around her for a place to hide. "Get under the table, quick," she hissed.

Salvu darted across the room and crawled behind the tablecloth. Lottie straightened out the parchments on the desk, then joined him.

Seconds later the door opened and two men walked in.

"Someone's been in here," said Captain Dragut's voice immediately.

"Maybe it was one of the lads cleaning out your vases," said a second, slightly softer voice.

"I had the door locked," insisted Dragut. "Whoever the culprit was must have climbed in through the window. There's a streak of mud on the sill – look."

"Mud?" said the softer voice. "But no one's been on shore today. How could there be mud?"

There was a long silence, during which Captain Dragut marched around the cabin, picking up things and dropping them angrily on the carpet.

"Someone's been through my charts," he bellowed.

"Th . . .there . . . must be stowaways on the sh . . .ship, then," the softer voice stammered. "Shall I order a search?"

"Immediately."

The second man left the cabin. Captain Dragut bolted his window. Then he marched out of the cabin and locked the door behind him.

Salvu lifted the tablecloth a fraction and breathed a sigh of relief. "Don't worry, Lot," he said. "Mark should blow the lamp out long before Dragut comes back."

Lottie rubbed her numb feet. She was getting cramp, squeezed in such a small, uncomfortable space. "Can't we make a dash for it?" she asked.

"It's too risky," Salvu said. "There's pirates crawling all over the place. Listen."

Outside, there did seem to be a big palaver going on. People ran past the locked window. Footsteps echoed on the planks.

"I'm scared," Lottie confessed. "I'm glad we'll be out of here soon."

Suddenly a bell started to peal shrilly and Captain Dragut's voice echoed round the ship.

"What's he saying?" Lottie asked.

"They've found a boy in the store room," Salvu whispered, his face going deathly pale. "He's clutching a lighted lamp."

7. The Witch's Pictures

There was a sweet smell of incense in the little vault tucked away behind the stern of the *Growling Dragon II*. Small, yellow candles guttered in front of a statue of the goddess Astarte. A glass bead curtain moved and tinkled in the faint breeze.

Captain Dragut studied his three prisoners suspiciously. "How did you climb aboard my ship?" he growled, his voice reminding Salvu of a deadly panther he had once seen at the circus.

Lottie and Mark, unable to understand Arabic, were silent. Salvu forced a smile and looked the pirate straight in the eyes. "We are escaped slaves," he lied, hoping Dragut would believe him. "We climbed aboard your ship, intending to flee the island."

Captain Dragut threw a glance at the second

man in the vault, then looked at Salvu again.

"And the lamp?"

"We found it in the sea while diving for cuttle-fish," Salvu said. "We didn't know it belonged to you."

Dragut fondled the lamp lovingly. "It does. And now that I've found it once more, I shall never let the light go out again."

Salvu heard Lottie stifle a gasp behind him. "We're glad we've found it for you, Captain," he said quickly. "Maybe we could be of some other service before we continue our journey?"

"*Continue* your journey?" Captain Dragut fixed Salvu with a malicious gleam in his eye. "Your journey ends here, my friends, your journey ends here."

Abruptly he turned to his assistant and tossed him a bunch of keys. "Lock these wretches in the store room," he ordered. "Two of them have a fair skin. They'll fetch a high price in the slave markets of Egypt."

The assistant caught the keys and bowed. Dragut started talking to him in a strange dialect, pointing at the lamp all the time.

Lottie turned on Mark. "Why didn't you blow the lamp out when you were caught?" she hissed.

"I couldn't," Mark complained. "The pirates snatched it away before I even knew what was happening."

"Stop it, you two," Salvu cut in. "Don't speak

45

at all. And don't move. I'll try to get us locked in here so we can blow the lamp out."

"Can't we do it now?" Mark sounded very scared.

"We're too far away from it," Salvu said. "I've got a better idea. Lottie, have you still got the first photograph Mark took in the haunted cave?"

Lottie dug in her pockets. "Sure, but it's all crumpled now."

"Never mind," Salvu said, slipping the picture under his belt. He waited until Captain Dragut had left the room. Then he turned to the assistant and smiled.

"You are Yusuf Sayid, aren't you?" he asked.

"What of it?" snapped the man.

"Sometimes you go alone to a cave in Gozo," Salvu continued. "You drink water from a well there."

"Am I so renowned in Gozo that all my movements are known by children?" laughed Yusuf.

"Sometimes we go to the same cave," Salvu said. "The master we escaped from is a wizard. He believes the water in that well has magical powers."

"Does he now?" asked Yusuf sarcastically.

"Our master made a contraption," Salvu bluffed. "It can make enchanted pictures – not pictures of our time, but pictures of the future. When he made a picture of the cave around the well, we saw your grave in it."

"He must be mistaken," Yusuf said gruffly, "I am to be buried at sea. It is written in my will."

"I'm afraid your wishes will not be honoured," Salvu warned. "Dragut will wound you at sea, and you will die in the cave."

Yusuf jangled the keys impatiently. "Enough of this nonsense," he spat. "Dragut has made me his right hand man. He will not kill me."

"Our master's magic does not lie," Salvu insisted. "If you lock us in here instead of the store room, we'll show you the picture."

"You only want to lay your hands on the lamp again," Yusuf laughed. "Do you think I am a fool not to notice such plans?"

"We cannot escape, can we?" Salvu begged. "You have nothing to fear."

"I don't trust you," Yusuf said.

"Why?" Salvu's eyes were fixed on Yusuf's now. "Do you believe we can escape by magical means?"

Yusuf looked away, his eyes betraying a slight hint of uncertainty. "I don't believe in witch-craft."

"You do," Salvu cut in quickly. "My master told me you often buy potions from the bazaars in Alexandria."

Yusuf was silent for a moment.

"See the picture for yourself," Salvu said. He took the photograph from under his belt and offered it to Yusuf. The pirate grabbed it roughly. He ran his fingers over its smooth surface. Then he turned it round and examined the blank space on the back.

"Look at the gravestone closely," Salvu continued. "Isn't that your name on it?"

Yusuf stared at the picture for a long time. When he looked up again, there was an unmistakable hint of fear in his eyes.

"There is no date on this gravestone," he said. "How am I to know when I'm going to die?"

"We can tell you," Salvu said. "But for that piece of information we want another favour."

Yusuf looked as if he might lose his patience any time. "What is it that you require this time?" he snapped.

"The map to the Sant's family treasure," Salvu said brazenly.

Yusuf was so startled, he was lost for words. "It's quite impossible," he hissed at last.

"Then I'm afraid you'll get no more information out of us," Salvu said.

"You are very courageous, witch's boy," Yusuf laughed lamely. "Dragut has some very impressive pieces of torture machinery to help extract information from spies and traitors like you." He dipped his hand under his sash and pulled out a scroll. "Still, you can't look for the treasure while you're locked up, can you? It will do no harm if you keep the map until you're sold in Egypt."

He handed the scroll to Salvu.

"Even if you did find the treasure, you'd never get out of its hiding place alive," he said.

"Never mind that," Salvu said. "The date on the gravestone is . . ."

His words were interrupted by footsteps.

"Hide the map," Yusuf hissed.

Salvu thrust the scroll under his belt. A moment later a pirate marched into the room. "Captain Dragut wants you to sort out some trouble in the galleys," he said. "I'll take the children to his cabin."

Yusuf left without another word. The pirate grabbed the children and hustled them out of the vault.

"Let go of us," Salvu protested.

The pirate tightened his hold on Salvu's collar and lifted him right off his feet. Salvu felt his elbow brush against the pirate's chest. He kicked frantically.

Mark closed his eyes. In this moment of despair, he had found courage inside him he never knew he had. Lifting his arm in the air, he punched their captor right in the stomach. The man yelped with pain and doubled over.

Salvu felt the tight hold on his collar loosen. Quick as lightning, he turned and dealt the pirate a blow on the back of the neck. He collapsed immediately. Salvu grabbed the man's dagger and turned to the others. "Quick," he said. "Let's dive overboard while we can."

The three ran to the edge of the deck. Mark dived into the sea without a thought but Salvu and Lottie stopped for a moment.

"Give me the second photograph, quick," Salvu whispered.

Lottie pulled the crumpled picture out of her pocket. Salvu pinned it to the deck with the pirate's dagger. Then he plunged after Lottie into the water below.

"I hope Yusuf finds the photograph," Lottie spluttered as the children swam towards the shore.

"I hope so too," Salvu said. "The twenty-sixth of August is tomorrow."

8. Treasure Hunt

"What do we do now?" Mark asked.

Salvu looked at the square around him. He and his friends had walked inland to Rabat, the walled capital city of Gozo that had been built by the Knights as a shelter from the pirates. After escaping from Captain Dragut and his henchmen, the three had been fed and given a warm bed for the night by some farmers. Now they were sitting on a stone bench in Tokk Square, the very centre of Rabat.

"I think we should try and find the treasure before Captain Dragut finds out we've got the map," Lottie said.

"Yes," Salvu agreed. "Then, somehow, we've got to find a way of putting out the lamp."

"And if we can't find it?" Mark asked. "We'll be stuck in the past for ever, won't we?"

Salvu shrugged. "Why don't we try and solve one problem at a time?" he suggested.

"Right," Lottie said. "Let's have a look at that map."

Salvu unrolled the scroll and spread it on his knees. The map didn't look like a real map at all. It had no drawing of Gozo or any other island on it. Instead, it had a curious picture of a cross cut up into rows of equal rectangles, each of which was filled with a picture of a grinning skeleton. The skeletons were all alike, except for one right in the middle of the map which had a flower drawn over one rib and a diamond between its hands.

To make matters more confusing, the cross's border had four small gaps in it, one at every end of the cross.

"I can't figure it out," Salvu said. "What on earth could it mean?"

"It could be the plan of some big cross somewhere," Mark wondered. "Maybe the treasure is hidden inside a cross."

"Let me have a proper look," Lottie said. She took the map from Salvu, smoothed it down on her lap and looked at it for a long time.

"This looks like a floor plan of a building to me," she said at last. "We did a project about buildings last year with Miss Potts. The floor plans all had gaps like this to show where the doors should be."

"What building would be built like a cross?" Mark asked.

"A church," Salvu cried. "That's the floor plan of a church. Churches are often built in the shape of a cross, aren't they?"

"What are the rectangles, then?" Lottie enquired.

"Graves," Salvu said triumphantly. "That's the map of Rabat Cathedral."

"Is that full of graves?"

Salvu grinned. "The whole floor is covered in them."

Lottie jumped off the bench. "Let's go and have a look right away," she cried.

"Control yourself," Salvu laughed. "People are staring at us."

Lottie calmed down and stuffed the map back into her pocket.

"All right", Salvu said. "Let's go."

The three of them crossed the road behind the square and started walking in the direction of the cathedral. Rabat is a very small town. All its roads lead from the surrounding farms, past the town houses to the cathedral on the hill.

Salvu chose the quickest way through a sunlit alley with vines hanging from balcony to balcony. It didn't take them very long to reach their destination.

"It's almost lunchtime," Salvu said as they pushed open the door and entered the cathedral.

"There shouldn't be many people around."

"Ugh," Lottie cried. "I can't see a thing."

Salvu put his arm on her shoulder. "Wait a bit," he said. "Your eyes will soon get used to the darkness."

They stood still for a moment, waiting for their eyes to adjust to the gloom around them. When they could make out a huge altar decorated with white geraniums and red candles at the far end of the church, they sat down on a pew and Lottie pulled the map out of her pocket again.

"If this is the right church, there must be forty rows of graves stretching from the west door to the east door behind the altar," Salvu said.

Lottie put the map on Mark's lap and stood up. "Shall I count them?" she asked.

Salvu nodded. Lottie went back to the west door they had come through. She chose a grave with a marble picture of a winged horse and stepped on it. The marble was cool under her feet. Lottie tried to read the writing on the grave but the words were all in French. The only thing she could make out was the name of the person buried under her feet – Maurice Flaubert.

Just then an old woman came into the church and knelt at the back pew behind Mark and Salvu. Lottie started counting, moving slowly along the graves as if she was admiring the paintings and sculptures around her. When she reached the far end of the church, she stopped for a moment to admire the magnificent organ covering the entire wall behind the altar and then returned to the boys.

"There are forty rows exactly," she whispered.

The boys looked pleased. "The skeleton with the flower on his rib should be in the middle of the twenty-fifth row," Salvu said.

The woman at the back pew rattled her rosary beads angrily and the children stopped talking. The woman crossed herself. Then she stood up, glared at the children and left.

"Let's go now," Mark said.

All three of them went to the west door again and started counting. The twenty-fifth row of graves turned out to be directly in front of the altar.

"There's no skeleton in the middle one," Lottie said, pointing to a grave decorated with a colour-ful mosaic of a young woman holding a lamb. "We must have done something wrong."

"Maybe it's under the altar," Mark suggested.

Salvu consulted the map. "No, the altar is covering the six middle graves of the twenty-seventh and twenty-eighth rows."

"What do we do now?" asked Lottie.

"We'll have to sit down and think about it," Salvu said.

To their right the sacristy door creaked open and an old man in a cotton shirt and grey trousers shuffled into the cathedral.

"That must be the sacristan," Salvu whispered. "Come on, let's go back to our seats."

The sacristan climbed the few steps leading to the altar and started picking out the drooping geraniums from the vases. The children hurried to the back pew and sat down. The sacristan finished plucking the flowers, then started the long job of sharpening the guttering candles.

Salvu closed his eyes and tried to think. What were they doing wrong? Were they counting the graves right? Were they, in fact, looking in the right place? There could be other churches in Gozo with graves in the floor. And they had no definite proof that the treasure was buried on the island, either. It could easily be in Malta, or Sicily, or any of the other Mediterranean islands Dragut attacked so often.

Suddenly Salvu felt a sharp nudge in the ribs. "Hey," Mark whispered in his ear. "Have you noticed this?"

Salvu opened his eyes. "Noticed what?"

"The writing on the graves," said Mark. "The first five rows are in French. All the others have Latin inscriptions."

"What difference does that make?" Lottie asked.

"It means the graves back here were added to the cathedral after Dragut buried his treasure,"

Salvu gasped. "The knights who built the original graves always used Latin in church."

"And the five rows of graves at the east end of the church could be hidden under the organ," Lottie said. "You can't really tell because the thing stretches right across the wall."

Salvu looked at the map again. "If that's right, then the grave we want is really in the thirtieth row from the west not the twenty-fifth."

"That's two rows behind the altar," Mark said. "No wonder we couldn't see it."

At the other end of the church, the sacristan finished sharpening the candles and carried the shavings out. Lottie looked at the French graves. Yes, the mortar round the edges of the marble slabs was white and new. They could only have been there for a couple of months.

"Why didn't I think of it before?" Salvu said. "We're in 1565 now. The new Grandmaster of the Island is Jean De LaValette, a Frenchman. It's obvious that he would want any new graves dug during his reign to have their inscriptions carved in French."

Mark took the map from Salvu and started counting. "There should be twelve graves stretching along row thirty," he informed the others. "The one we need is number seven, starting from the left."

Salvu took the lead and his friends followed him round the altar to the vestry at the back.

Here the shadows were deeper than in the rest of the cathedral. The walls were lined with oak panelling. Small tallow candles burned at a niche in one corner.

Lottie walked to the left wall, turned and started counting the graves. "This is it," she said, stopping at the seventh grave.

Mark and Salvu looked at the tomb. It wasn't flush with the ground like the others. Instead it was raised like a deathbed with a bronze skeleton on top.

"We've found it," Salvu shouted, unable to keep his voice down with all the excitement. "Now – we'll have to figure out what the flower on the rib means."

"Maybe we should just press the rib," Mark said.

Salvu pressed it, but nothing happened. "There isn't enough light in here," he muttered. "Mark, bring me a candle, could you?"

Mark fetched one of the candles from the niche and held it above the tomb.

"That's better," Salvu said. He inspected the rib closely. There was nothing to suggest it was any different from the other bones on the skeleton.

"Maybe we should clean it up a bit," Lottie ventured. "We can't really see anything with all the dust on the tomb." She took a handkerchief from her pocket, spat on it and started rubbing away at the skeleton's rib.

"I can see a crack underneath it now," Salvu said. "I think this rib could be a lever." He tried pulling it up but his fingers kept slipping.

"Let me try," Lottie offered, pushing him aside. She closed her fingers round the lever and pulled until her hand slipped too. The rib only came up a fraction.

"Why don't we prise it up with something?"

Salvu dug in his pocket for a five-cent piece. He wedged the edge of the coin under the rib and twisted it. The rib came up some more. There was enough space for someone to get a proper hold of it now. Lottie closed her fingers round it and pulled it right up without any trouble.

For a moment nothing happened. Then something inside the grave started to rumble. A big crack spread from the skeleton's skull right down to its toes.

"We've done it!" Mark gasped.

The crack in the skeleton widened, releasing a stench of mildew and rotting wood. The tomb's surface split in two complete parts and opened up like the flaps on a gigantic cardboard box.

Clouds of thick, choking dust rose out of the grave, filling the air and dimming Mark's candle. Salvu clapped his hands over his mouth and peered over the edge of the tomb. In the darkness he could make out a flight of stairs.

"Come on," he told the others. "The treasure must be down there."

Cautiously, the three of them climbed over the skeleton and descended the stairs. Mice and beetles scurried away from their feet, as they tore a huge tunnel in a curtain of webs. At last they reached the bottom of the stairs and found themselves in a small chamber hewn out of rock.

Mark's candle flickered dangerously and almost went out. Salvu took it from him and placed it carefully on a rock. The flame sputtered, then steadied itself and threw a feeble light upon the walls. The children looked around them.

"This must be an ancient crypt," Salvu whispered. "Look we're surrounded by crumbling skeletons."

"Where's the treasure?" Mark asked.

Salvu picked up the candle and held it carefully above a circular stone right in the middle of the crypt. "It should be in here," he said.

Lottie knelt by the stone. "Is this a millstone?"

"No, it's an *agape* table, an altar." Salvu ran his fingers lightly round the edge of the stone, feeling the smoothness of the carving. "Early Christians used to come here for the breaking of the bread. They had to worship in hiding because Christianity was illegal then. They called their feast the *agape* and this was their table."

"Did they build it especially?" Mark asked.

Salvu shook his head. "No, the table was used even before the Christians. People of many ancient religions had meals in honour of the dead. The followers of Christ merely adapted old customs to fit their new faith."

"Does the table open?" Lottie wondered.

"It does. People used to keep jugs and platters inside. It was like having a table and a sideboard rolled into one."

"Let's see if the treasure is inside it," Mark said.

They lifted the stone lid and propped it against a wall. Then they returned to the table. There was nothing inside it, except a cracked jug half-buried in a layer of dust and sand.

"We've been tricked," Lottie groaned.

"Maybe Yusuf gave us the wrong map," Mark added.

Salvu said nothing. He reached for the jug and lifted it. The ancient pottery fell apart in his hand. Bits of clay fell back into the dust. Salvu brushed them away with his hand and uncovered a tiny mosaic of a squatting, headless woman.

"Astarte," Salvu whispered, pressing on the mosaic's broken neck with his thumb.

Suddenly, the table shuddered. Its bottom fell away, revealing a shallow pit. Salvu shone the candle over it. Something in the dark picked up the light and flashed it back. Salvu narrowed his eyes to see better. There, sitting on the bottom, lay an open chest full of gold and diamonds.

"We've found it!" Mark gasped. "We've found the treasure."

9. *The Haunted Well Again*

The children buried the treasure in a new hiding place at half past four in the afternoon, while most of the people on Gozo were still locked indoors having their siesta. After locating the gold and diamonds, Salvu had crept out of the church and taken three pillow cases from the washing line of a nearby house. As payment he left a gold coin in the pockets of a drying apron.

"I think we should hide the treasure in our cave," Lottie had said. "That way we'll stand a better chance of finding it when we go back to our time."

"Good thinking," Salvu agreed. "The cliffs of Pudding Beach are not far from here either."

They hurried out of the church and made their way along the narrow streets, past old farms that they knew would still be standing in the twentieth century. Soon they reached the cliffs leading to the Sant villa and started the long trek up the rocks.

Once on top, they stopped to regain their breath. "Look," Mark said. "The villa looks exactly the same as it does in our time."

Salvu stared at the ivy-covered walls. It was strange looking at a place that would one day be your own home, he thought. Mark nudged him in the ribs and he turned round to see several people walking around the harbour below.

"We'd better hurry," Lottie said. "Siesta time seems to be over."

"They crossed the rocks towards the villa and found the door to the cellar. Someone had already been there after Captain Dragut's attack. There was some orange peel on the floor and the doors of a few rabbit hutches had been stolen, probably for firewood.

Lottie made straight for the ancient trapdoor buried under the debris. Mark helped her remove the stones and open the door.

"Come on," Lottie said. "Let's put these gems away for safekeeping."

She led the boys down the steps and along the tunnel until they reached the cave. Salvu stopped to look around him. "It's almost exactly like it is in our time, isn't it?" he said.

Lottie agreed. She knelt on the ground and started digging in the soft sand with her bare hands. The boys joined her and in no time at all they had dug a deep, narrow pit.

Salvu lowered the pillow cases in and helped the others heap the sand back in place. When they had finished, they left the cave and closed the trapdoor at the end of the tunnel.

It was almost six now but the day was still hot.

"Why don't we go to the haunted well and get a drink of water?" Mark suggested.

"Yes, let's," Salvu said.

They hurried down the cliffs and took the road that led away from the harbour. Then they turned right, crossed an empty field and started along a familiar dirt track.

Lottie saw a pomegranate tree in front of them and hurried to pick some fruit.

"Hey," she called. "There's blood on the ground."

"It must be a hedgehog," Mark called back. "Been run over by a car or something."

Lottie laughed, picked an overripe fruit and threw it at her brother.

"You dumbo," she said.

"Okay," Mark sighed. "A cart, then."

"Or a coach," said Salvu. "They called it a *kaless* in the 1560s, I believe."

"There's more blood," Lottie shouted. "It must have been a very big hedgehog."

"Maybe it was a cow," Mark said. "Come on, I'll race you both to the well. I'm dying of thirst."

The three of them broke into a run towards the old farm. "Hey, it's only a little hut," Mark said. "There's no farm yet."

Lottie pushed past the boys and dived through a curtain of fronds into the cave. It was cool around the well, and almost dark after the harsh glare of the sun. Lottie looked around and found a pitcher.

"Let me fill it up," Mark said.

He picked it up and plunged it into the water. Behind him, someone moaned softly. The children stiffened, turned.

"There's someone in that corner," Lottie said.

The person moved, and a small diamond caught the light.

"Yusuf," Salvu gasped.

The pirate rose slowly on his elbows and tried to smile. His skin was deathly pale, as if all the blood in his body had drained out.

"You're wounded," Salvu said.

Yusuf nodded. "Your master was right after all," he whispered. "Dragut wasn't my friend."

Salvu tore a piece off his shirt, dipped it in the pitcher of water and put it to the pirate's brow. "Did he find out you gave us the map?" he asked.

Yusuf rested his head on the ground. "No, he accused me of stealing gold from his coffers. We argued, and he ran me through with his sword."

"The pig," Lottie said.

Yusuf took the girl's hand and his lips trembled in a deathly whisper. "He must be stopped. Otherwise there will be no end to this bloodshed. Do you understand?"

"What can we do?" Salvu asked.

"Go to the Knights of Malta," Yusuf said. "They've been hunting Dragut for the past twenty years. If they can corner him in a harbour, he'll stand no chance. His hiding place is the Bay of Ragusa in Sicily."

Salvu took the cloth from the pirate's head and wrung it out. "Can we get the lamp back, do you think?"

Yusuf removed a ruby ring from his finger and handed it to Lottie. "Take this to the Grandmaster on the island of Malta. He will recognise it as one of the rings Dragut stole from a Cardinal of Rome. It will be your proof. Bargain with him. Say you will show him the way to Dragut's hideout only if he takes you with him so that you can get the lamp back. The Grandmaster is an honest man. He will not betray you."

Lottie slipped the ring on her finger and smiled. Yusuf moved his arm again with great difficulty and reached for a purse in his tunic. "You must buy me a tombstone," he said. "A soul without a grave cannot rest properly."

"You're not going to die, yet," Lottie cried. "Hold on a bit and we'll get help. We'll take you to a hospital."

Yusuf smiled weakly. "I shall always be here if you need me," he whispered. Then he was still. Outside the wind rustled through the trees and the crickets sang their mournful afternoon song.

"He's gone," Lottie said sadly.

Mark stretched Yusuf's body out on the ground and folded his cold arms on his chest.

Towards evening the three of them went to a mason's and ordered a grave to be dug in the cave and a tombstone to be erected above it.

The mason's apprentice asked them what writing they wanted on the stone and they repeated the inscription they had photographed only a day before:

HERE LIES
YUSUF SAYID
MURDERED BY HIS OWN CAPTAIN
OLAF DRAGUT
ON THE 26TH OF AUGUST 1565
MAY GOD HAVE MERCY ON HIS SOUL

10. Meeting the Grandmaster

"I don't believe it," Mark cried. "We get the map. We find the treasure. And now we can't even get into the palace to see the Grandmaster."

"Maybe we ought to hitch a lift to Ragusa and try to get the lamp ourselves," Lottie suggested.

"We'll never make it without the Knights of Malta," Salvu said wearily. "Dragut will just catch us again."

Mark scowled and kicked at the dust on the street. "Perhaps we could wait for the Grandmaster outside the palace. He's got to come out sooner or later."

"Yeah. But he'll probably be in one of those carriages with velvet curtains," Lottie said. "I think our best bet is to corner him in some public place."

"You're right," Salvu cried. "Why don't we

go to the market and find out where he goes to church?"

They left the palace square and took a shortcut through the side streets into the market.

"It's amazing how Birgu hasn't changed a bit in over four hundred years," Salvu said. "Even the shops seem to have the same fronts as in our time."

Lottie spied a fruit stall and they bought sweet ripe melons sprinkled with ginger.

"Are you in town for the fireworks?" the stallkeeper asked.

"What fireworks, *habiba*?" Salvu dug for the last of Yusuf's money in his pocket.

"The ones in the harbour tonight, dear," the stallkeeper snorted patiently. "Where have you been these last few days? On the moon?"

"We've just come over from Gozo on a produce boat," Salvu said.

"Ah," the woman nodded. "Then you should stay the night in the city, dear. The Grandmaster is giving a firework display in honour of the visiting Cardinal this evening. There's going to be a boat race across the harbour later, and a ball for the hoity-toity in the palace."

"Is there?" A grin spread across Salvu's face. "I wonder if the Grandmaster himself is going to be there?"

The woman flicked flies away from her fruit with a rag. "The Grandmaster? Of course. The

Grandmaster never misses a ball or a fête, dear."

"Then we musn't either," Salvu laughed. "You've been most helpful, *habiba*."

The stallkeeper smiled kindly. "That's all right, dear. Here's your change."

A man in a wide–brimmed hat approached the stall and the fruitseller turned to serve him. Salvu and his friends wandered off.

"What was the woman on about?" Lottie asked Salvu, her mouth full of melon.

"The Grandmaster is giving a fireworks display tonight," Salvu said. "We should investigate."

Mark finished his melon and wiped his fingers on his shirt. It was almost seven in the evening now and most of the market sellers were closing their stalls for the night.

"What do you say we go and watch them set up the fireworks?" he asked the others.

Salvu and Lottie agreed. So they left the market and walked along the narrow streets to the harbour.

The fireworks display was to take place on a small barge floating on the water. The children watched a crowd of young boys in white uni-forms set up seats all along the quay. On the barge itself several men were setting up poles with Catherine-wheels and draping them with long gunpowder fuses.

"Don't we know that man from somewhere?" Lottie said, pointing to a young, dark–haired man lashing sparklers to a wheel.

"That's one of the pirates from the *Growling Dragon II*," Salvu gasped. "No, he's not – he's the lookout on the *Growling Dragon II*."

"What's he doing here?" Lottie wondered.

"I don't know, but I'm sure he's up to no good."

"Should we warn the Grandmaster?" Mark asked.

Salvu shook his head. "We can't get to see him, can we? It's best if we wait here and see what happens."

"That bloke's taking a long time over that firework," Lottie said. "The rest are all finished."

"That thing he's working on is called 'the fountain'," Salvu explained. "It's usually the climax of the whole display."

The attendants in white cordoned off the seats with a velvet rope and retired to a caravan at the end of the harbour.

Salvu led his friends to the edge of the waterfront. "We stand a better chance of grabbing the Grandmaster's attention from here," he said. "He might even pass by us if we're lucky."

"Fat chance," Lottie said. "The way the place is filling up, we're going to be miles away from him."

"Hey, look," Mark whispered. "Our lookout is pacing around like a caged tiger. I wonder what he's waiting for."

74

All around, people started milling into the harbour. Some thrust their way towards the quay. Many others climbed on to the battlements on the other side of the harbour from where they could get a better view of the proceedings. Many of the Grandmaster's guests were shown to their comfortable chairs behind the velvet rope. The lookout found a seat very close to the barge and sat down.

Just before the display was about to start, there was a fanfare of trumpets and the Grandmaster arrived with his Italian visitors. Everyone present held their head high as a sign of respect, and the honourable group was led to a row of gilded chairs at the water's edge.

The attendants on the barge put a taper to the first firework and a score of blue Catherine-wheels burst into life.

The people roared their approval. The Catherine-wheels changed from blue to red and then to a fiery, dazzling gold. When they fizzled out, the attendants lit another taper, and a shower of sparklers zoomed across the sky, each little spark exploding into a web of fire in mid air. They were followed by golden cascades, and poles that burned in the shapes of fiery crowns and acrobats. The people oooed and aaahhed at every effect and the Italian visitors nodded their heads approvingly.

Then it was the turn of the Grandmaster to set

the last firework – the fountain of fire – alight. An attendant handed him a lighted taper and a knight led him to a small wooden jetty that reached out to the barge.

At the same time, Salvu looked around for the pirate lookout. He was not in his seat.

On the barge, the Grandmaster waved the lighted taper ceremoniously at the people. The crowd cheered and clapped. A flock of frightened gulls rose from the nearby trees, their beaks open in a shrill cry.

Salvu turned frantically and caught sight of the pirate lookout at the back of the crowd. There was a wild look to his sweating face and his eyes were fixed on the lighted taper.

Suddenly Salvu remembered the lookout's words on the *Growling Dragon II*: "*My brother has offered me a job with a band of mercenaries . . . they're planning something big . . . something that will have an explosive effect on the whole world . . .*"

"Stop, Your Highness," Salvu screamed, turning to the Grandmaster. "There is a bomb in that firework."

The Grandmaster froze, his hand only inches away from the firework's fuse. All the world seemed to go silent.

Then a knight stepped forward and pulled the Grandmaster away. Several guards stumbled aboard the barge and looked at the fountain of fire closely. From his position, Salvu could see

76

them throwing buckets of water on the fuse.

The Grandmaster turned to his guards and gestured with his hand. Suddenly everything became loud and noisy again. The guards dashed forward and snatched all the men on the boat. Salvu was swept towards the barge by a sea of curious people, all eager to have a peep at the ruined bomb.

Then a rough hand grabbed him by the shoulder and an angry voice bellowed in his ear. "Stay where you are, young man. You're under arrest."

11. The Clash with Dragut

A strong wind was rushing through the slackened sails of the *Maria Vittoria*, pulling the rigging taut and making the masts creak like wounded ghosts in an empty house.

"Here we are at last," Salvu said to Mark and Lottie. "Sailing the seas. Ready to pounce on Dragut."

"Yeah," Lottie laughed. "It was quite a bit of luck, us seeing the lookout and all, wasn't it?"

Salvu nodded. After his arrest the three of them had been taken to the palace for questioning. They described the lookout to the guards. They showed the Grandmaster Yusuf's ruby and told him how they could capture Captain Dragut. The Grandmaster agreed to their plan.

Now, after a clandestine departure from the Maltese harbour and a swift voyage that had been kept secret from even the highest officials on the island, the *Maria Vittoria* was waiting outside the Sicilian port of Ragusa, where the Grandmaster hoped to capture Dragut, disguised as an Arab merchant ship.

"The soldiers should be going over to Dragut's ship in a minute," Salvu said. "Then all we need do is get the lamp and – puff – we're back in our time with the treasure."

Just then the bigger sails on the midmast were pulled taut and the *Maria Vittoria* moved slowly forward.

"Watch out, Captain Dragut," Mark joked. "The pirates of Pudding Beach are coming to get you."

The children hurried to the prow and looked towards land. Salvu lifted a telescope to his eyes and studied the harbour. The *Growling Dragon II* was moored to the quay. Unfortunately she wasn't alone. Nine other schooners were tied up alongside it. Salvu put down his telescope. The knights had seen the extra ships too, for the sails were suddenly slackened and an anchor was swiftly dropped into the sea.

"Is there a problem?" Lottie said.

Salvu shrugged impatiently. "I don't know. But I guess we weren't expecting ten pirate ships."

"What do you reckon will happen now?" Mark wondered.

"I expect they'll send for more ships," Salvu said. "Or just plan a different ambush."

A sailor came rushing down the deck and told Salvu that the Grandmaster wanted to see him alone in his cabin. Salvu followed him towards the stern.

Meanwhile a group of knights and sailors started building a raft. They worked quickly, lashing the long planks together with ropes and twine and hemp.

A man in dark clothes came up from the ammunition store in the hold with a small powder keg on his shoulder.

"Stand back," he warned everyone.

The knights pushed the children gently back, and the powder keg was tied to the raft. Then a second keg was fetched and lashed on too. The man in the dark clothes tested the ropes to make sure the raft was safe, then he ordered the knights to lower it into the water.

The men handled it carefully, hissing at each other every time it bumped against the deck. When the raft was in the sea, they breathed a sigh of relief and waited.

A little later Salvu came out of the Grandmaster's cabin. He had oil smeared all over his arms, and his face had been blackened with soot.

"There's been some changes in the knights' plans," Salvu said. "The knights have not brought enough ammunition with them to attack the whole fleet. The only way they can get rid of Dragut is by blowing up his ship with the gunpowder on the raft. That man in the dark clothes is called Toni Bayada and he has agreed to take me over to the ship so I can get the lamp before the whole ship goes up in smoke."

"Will you blow it out before you come back?" Mark asked.

"It depends," Salvu replied. "If we find ourselves in danger, it's best to get out as quickly as we can."

"The whole thing sounds very dangerous to me," said Lottie. "But we haven't got any choice, have we?"

Salvu shook his head.

Mark patted him on the back. "Be careful, buddy," he said.

Salvu smiled and followed Toni Bayada down to the raft. The knights untied the rope that was securing it to the *Maria Vittoria*, and the swell picked it up.

"There's an oar behind you," Toni said in the dark.

Salvu found it and dipped its blade in the water. Paddling was easy for him. He had done it a thousand times before. Toni realised he had an expert on his hands. So he let Salvu steer the raft by himself while he sat by the powder kegs and made sure they didn't come loose.

At the far end of the harbour, the *Growling Dragon II* bobbed on the waves. A lantern flickered on the upper deck.

Salvu steered the raft quickly, crouching low all the time in case there was a lookout he could not see. The *Maria Vittoria* was left behind, and the large rocks that marked the entrance to the port of Ragusa loomed ahead.

Soon, the raft was nosing the prow of the *Growling Dragon II*. Toni stood up carefully. The raft wobbled dangerously and water slopped on to Salvu's shoes.

Toni beckoned for him to rise. He obeyed, taking care to keep his balance right. When he was standing, Toni picked up a rope and aimed it deftly at the railings above. The rope's noose caught on something Salvu couldn't see and held. Toni pulled it tight. He waited for a whole minute to make sure no one had seen or heard anything. Then, satisfied that the coast was clear, he gestured Salvu to climb aboard.

The boy shinnied up the rope without difficulty. Once on the deck he crouched in the shadows and looked around him. Captain Dragut's cabin lay to his left, the vault where the lamp was kept to his right.

The deck seemed deserted, but Salvu knew there was a watch prowling around somewhere. He made a dash for the old barrels on the upper deck and hid behind them until the guards had passed by. Then he inched his way towards the vault.

It was locked.

Suddenly, Salvu heard someone coming along the deck. He darted back behind the barrels and fixed his eyes on a gap between two of them. The prowler was Dragut, scowling and glaring as usual. Salvu saw him stop by the vault and fumble in his pocket for his large bunch of keys. Then the vault door creaked open.

Dragut did not go in. Instead, he stood still, the keys jangling against each other on their ring. The night seemed suddenly cold, and Salvu could hear his own breath rasping through his throat. Had he done something wrong? He looked down at his feet and stifled a gasp: water was seeping out of his shoes and spreading beyond the barrels.

Slowly, Salvu started backing away from the barrels. The jangling of Dragut's keys followed. "I've been caught," Salvu thought desperately. "What can I do?"

Suddenly there was a load roar. A large hand overturned the barrel next to Salvu and the boy leapt out.

"It's you again," hissed Captain Dragut in his face. "This time you shall not escape me, you fool."

He pulled his famous sword out of its sheath and swung it high over his head. Salvu backed away, his wet feet slipping on the worn planks. Dragut advanced, a cruel smile playing on his lips. Suddenly he shook his head, and his hair

fell around his face like a black waterfall. With a
wild yell, he leapt to a lantern hooked to a cabin
wall and thrust his sword into it. The blade came
away burning, dripping oil and flames.

Salvu covered his face with his hands. Inch
by slow, painful inch he backed across the deck.
His shoulders grazed against ropes and rigging
but he didn't feel anything. All he wanted to do
was escape from this madman, this ship. At last
he felt something hard poking his back: he was
right up against the railings.

Captain Dragut laughed and raised his flaming sword above his head once more. Salvu stole a glance over his shoulder. He couldn't jump into the sea: below him, Toni Bayada was struggling to push the raft away from the schooner. The powder kegs were bobbing dangerously.

Captain Dragut roared and brought his sword down. At the last moment Salvu jumped aside. The pirate cursed. His flaming sword hit the railings and went hurtling overboard.

Salvu saw Toni Bayada leap off the raft. He heard a massive explosion. A hot, searing wind blew him off his feet and he found himself thrown

up into the air. For a moment he saw the moon rushing down to meet him. The stars made a crazy pin-wheel in the sky. Then he closed his eyes against the stinging smoke and plunged back toward the cool, dark sea . . .

"Hey," Mark cried. "We're back in our cave."

Salvu opened his eyes. Far above him, the stalactites shone a phosphorescent green. Water dripped noisily into the pool.

"The explosion must have blown the lamp out," Lottie gasped. "Salv, are you all right?"

Salvu sat up slowly. "Just a bit shaken," he whispered. "I'll be fine in a minute."

Lottie smiled. "Phew, that was quite an adventure, wasn't it?" she said.

"It certainly was," Mark agreed.

Salvu picked up a handful of sand and threw it up in the air. "Who would believe it?" he laughed shakily. "We've been through all sorts of scrapes and adventures to get that treasure. And all the while it was lying right here at our feet."

Epilogue

The two fishermen caught the shark some ten miles to the north of Gozo. It was a Great White, with small, mean eyes and a huge mouth packed with sharp teeth.

"Let's clean it now," the younger of the two fishermen said.

He plunged his knife under the shark's jaw and ripped it open down to the tail. Steam rose from the warm flesh. Blood dripped on to the deck.

The older fisherman reached inside the shark and scooped out the innards. Whole squids and undigested fish spilled out with the guts. An old rubber boot followed, then an old lamp.

"Sharks are like pigs," the fisherman murmured. "They eat anything."

The younger fisherman picked up the lamp and wiped the blood away with his sleeve.

"Is this worth anything?" he asked.

The older one shook his head. "It's all Sicilian junk," he said. "The fish must have been rooting around the port of Ragusa. They say the seabed is full of wrecks there."

The younger one tossed the lamp into the sea. It sank to the bottom like a stone, its spout leaving a trail of bubbles in the water.

Later that evening a storm tossed it up again and carried it along on its currents. Soon it had reached the cliffs of Gozo and was pitched into an underwater cave.

Towards midnight the storm waned and dropped, and the lamp came to rest by the wreck of an old pirate ship.

All around it, the water was still.

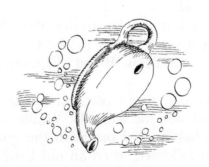